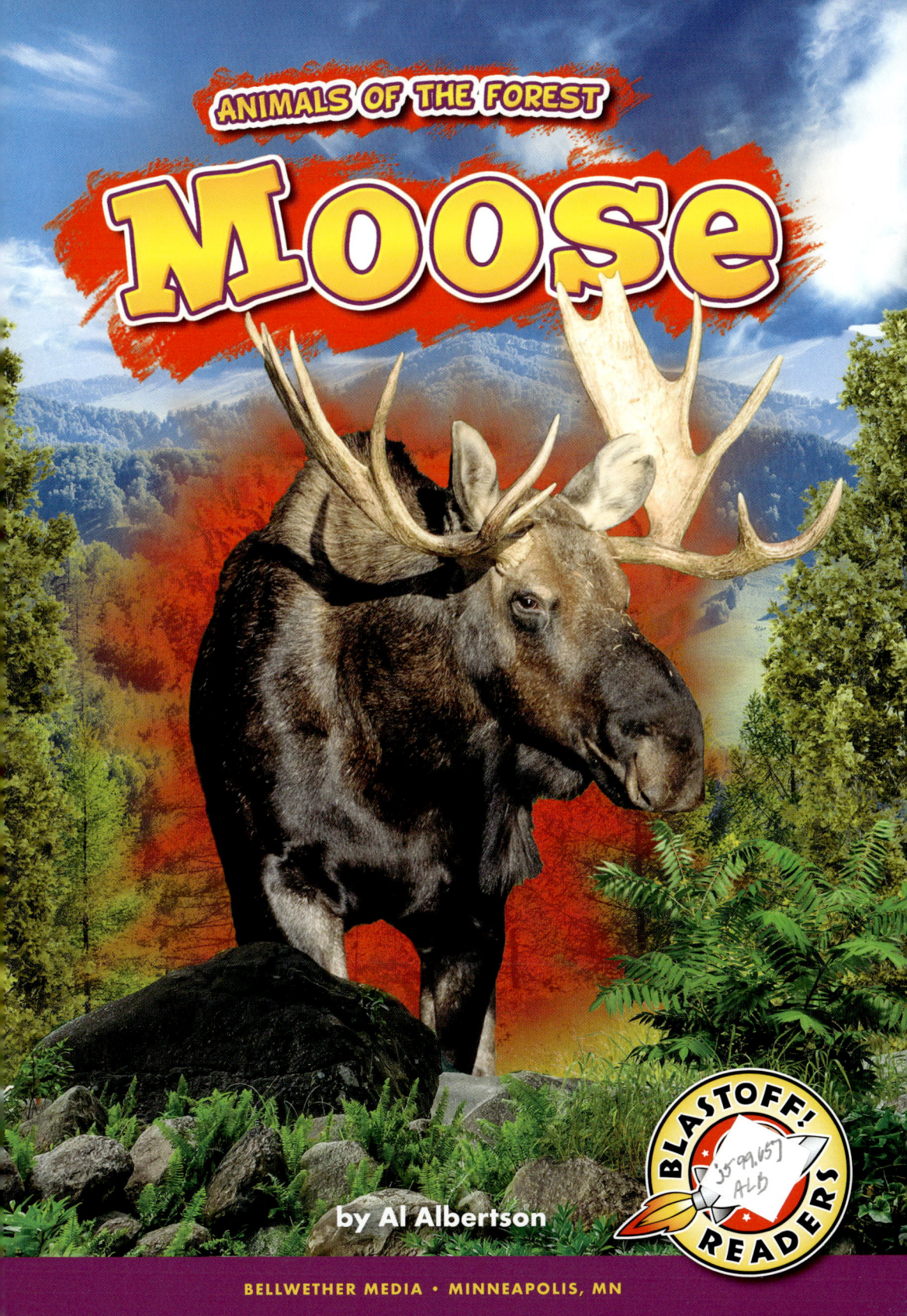

Animals of the Forest
Moose

by Al Albertson

BELLWETHER MEDIA • MINNEAPOLIS, MN

Note to Librarians, Teachers, and Parents:

Blastoff! Readers are carefully developed by literacy experts and combine standards-based content with developmentally appropriate text.

Level 1 provides the most support through repetition of high-frequency words, light text, predictable sentence patterns, and strong visual support.

Level 2 offers early readers a bit more challenge through varied simple sentences, increased text load, and less repetition of high-frequency words.

Level 3 advances early-fluent readers toward fluency through increased text and concept load, less reliance on visuals, longer sentences, and more literary language.

Level 4 builds reading stamina by providing more text per page, increased use of punctuation, greater variation in sentence patterns, and increasingly challenging vocabulary.

Level 5 encourages children to move from "learning to read" to "reading to learn" by providing even more text, varied writing styles, and less familiar topics.

Whichever book is right for your reader, Blastoff! Readers are the perfect books to build confidence and encourage a love of reading that will last a lifetime!

This edition first published in 2020 by Bellwether Media, Inc.

No part of this publication may be reproduced in whole or in part without written permission of the publisher. For information regarding permission, write to Bellwether Media, Inc., Attention: Permissions Department, 6012 Blue Circle Drive, Minnetonka, MN 55343.

Library of Congress Cataloging-in-Publication Data

Names: Albertson, Al, author.
Title: Moose / by Al Albertson.
Description: Minneapolis, MN : Bellwether Media, Inc., 2020. | Series: Blastoff! readers: animals of the forest | Includes bibliographical references and index. | Audience: Ages 5-8 | Audience: Grades K-1 | Summary: "Relevant images match informative text in this introduction to moose. Intended for students in kindergarten through third grade"-- Provided by publisher.
Identifiers: LCCN 2019024913 (print) | LCCN 2019024914 (ebook) | ISBN 9781644871287 (library binding) | ISBN 9781618918048 (ebook)
Subjects: LCSH: Moose--Juvenile literature.
Classification: LCC QL737.U55 A435 2020 (print) | LCC QL737.U55 (ebook) | DDC 599.65/7--dc23
LC record available at https://lccn.loc.gov/2019024913
LC ebook record available at https://lccn.loc.gov/2019024914

Text copyright © 2020 by Bellwether Media, Inc. BLASTOFF! READERS and associated logos are trademarks and/or registered trademarks of Bellwether Media, Inc.

Editor: Betsy Rathburn   Designer: Josh Brink

Printed in the United States of America, North Mankato, MN.

Table of Contents

Life in the Forest — 4
Antlers and Seasons — 10
Twigs and Leaves — 16
Glossary — 22
To Learn More — 23
Index — 24

Life in the Forest

Moose are big **mammals**. They live in northern forests around the world.

They are well **adapted** to this **biome**!

Moose Range

range =

Moose are prepared for forest winters. Long legs help them walk through deep snow.

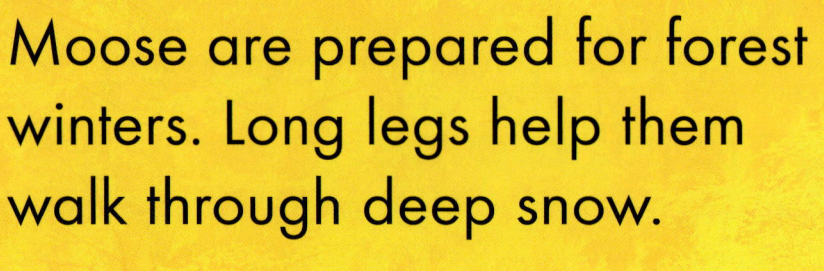

← guard hairs

Two layers of fur keep moose warm. **Guard hairs** lie over soft **underfur**.

The forest floor can be hard or soft. **Split hooves** help moose walk across any surface.

Special Adaptations

two layers of fur

long legs

split hooves

These hooves also help moose swim across rivers and lakes!

Antlers and Seasons

Moose wander large home **ranges**. They usually travel alone.

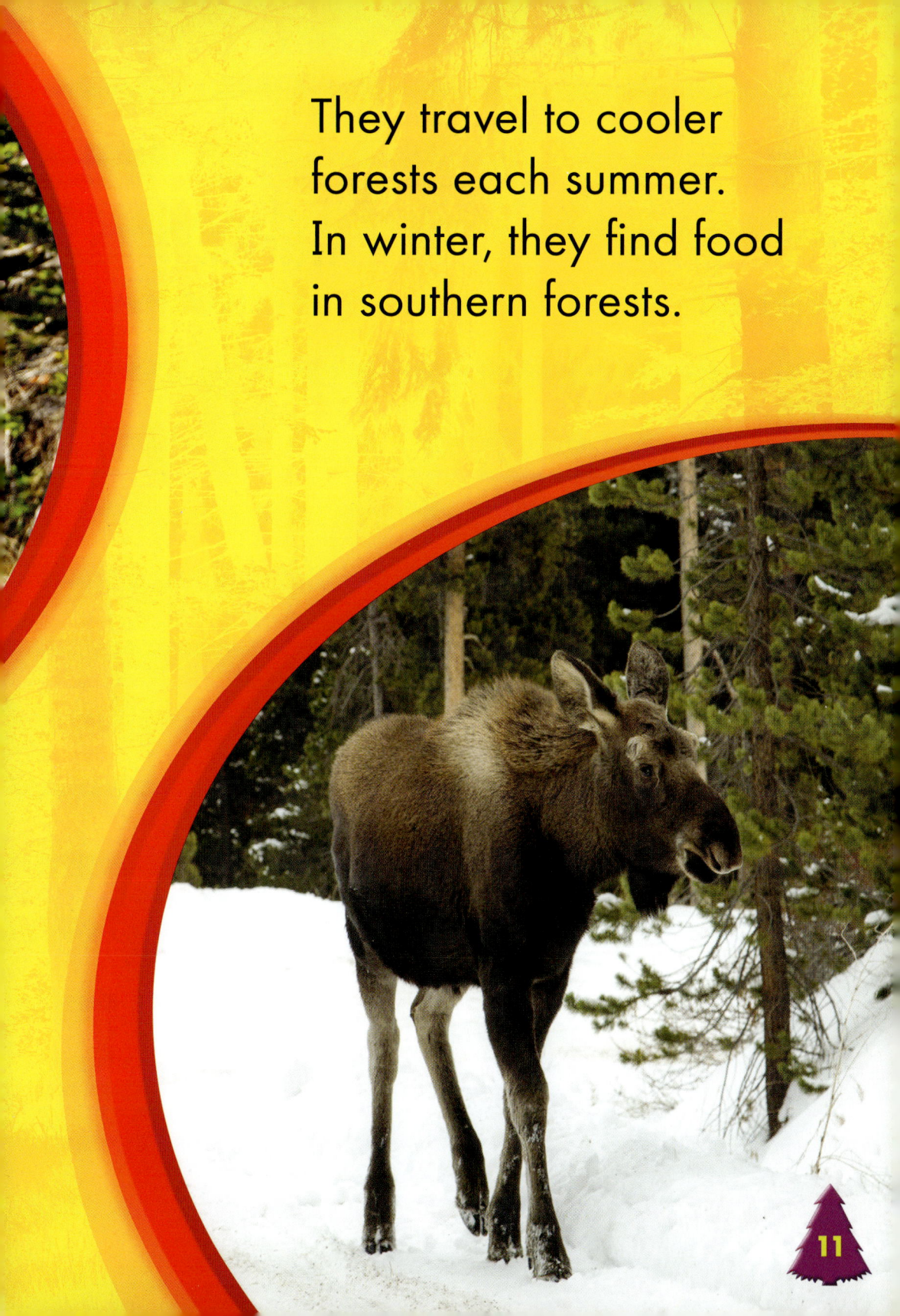

They travel to cooler forests each summer. In winter, they find food in southern forests.

Male moose begin to grow **antlers** each spring. Antlers help them find **mates**.

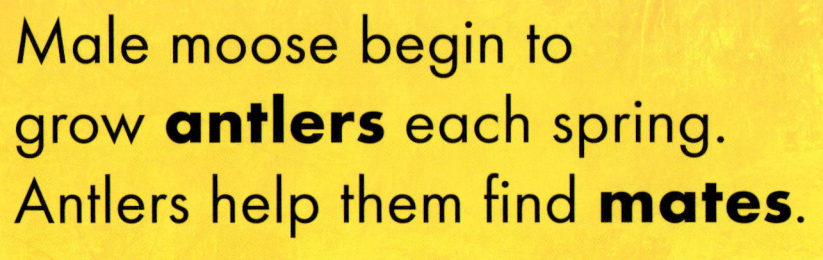

antlers

Big antlers also scare off forest **predators**. Moose **charge** at bears, wolves, and other enemies!

Moose antlers grow through the summer. They can reach 6 feet (2 meters) across!

In winter, moose lose their antlers. This helps save **energy** for the cold season ahead.

Moose Stats

| Least Concern | Near Threatened | Vulnerable | Endangered | Critically Endangered | Extinct in the Wild | Extinct |

conservation status: least concern

life span: up to 20 years

Twigs and Leaves

Moose are **herbivores**. They munch on twigs and tree bark.

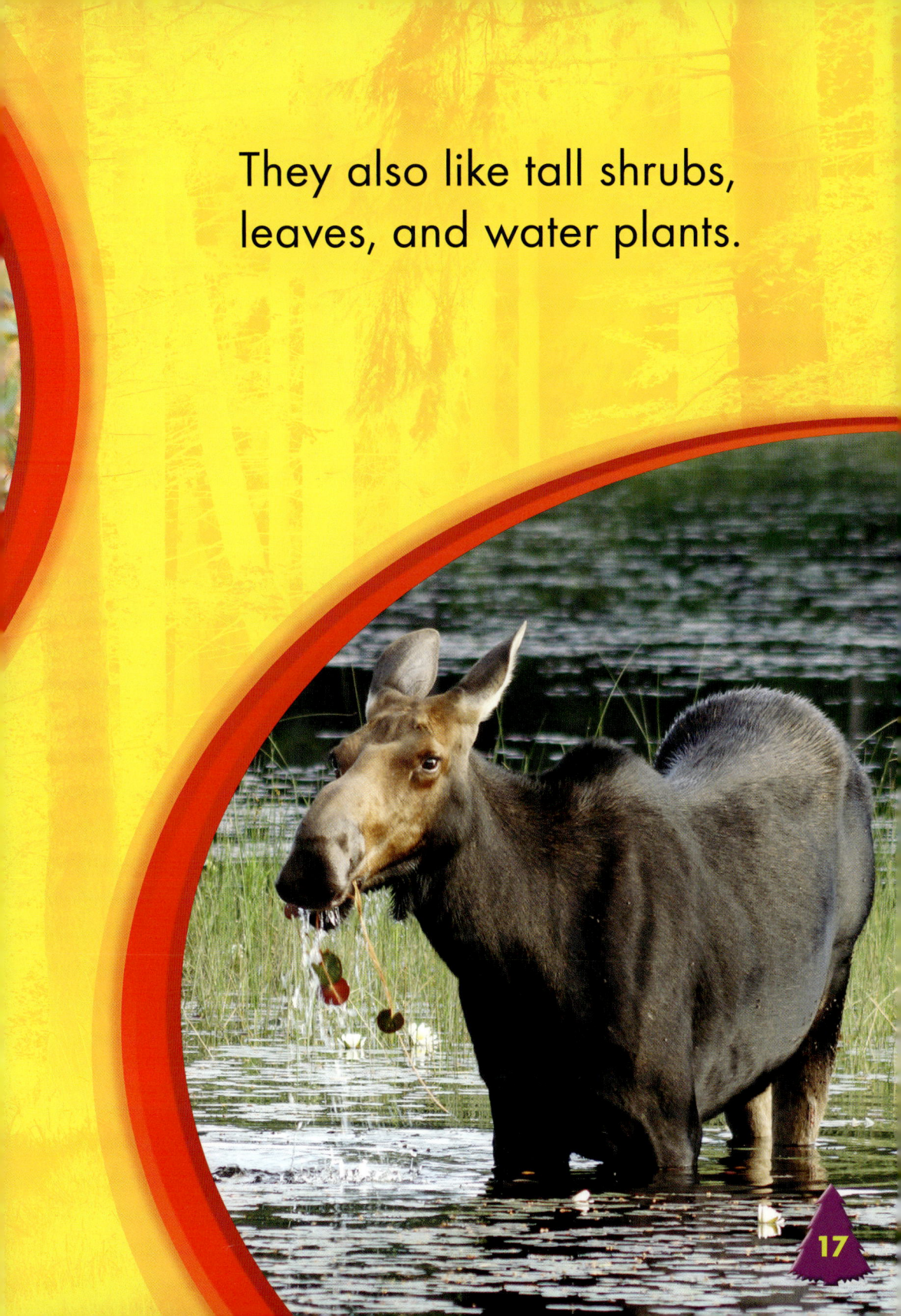

They also like tall shrubs, leaves, and water plants.

Moose do not have upper front teeth.

They pull leaves from trees with their bottom teeth and upper lip!

Moose Diet

aspen tree twigs

willow leaves

water lilies

Moose eat up to 60 pounds (27 kilograms) of food every day.

Sometimes food is hard to find. But moose know how to survive in the forest!

Glossary

adapted—well suited due to changes over a long period of time

antlers—branched bones on the heads of some animals; antlers look like horns.

biome—a large area with certain plants, animals, and weather

charge—to run at something fast with antlers pointed forward

energy—the power to move and do things

guard hairs—long, thick hairs on the outside of a moose's coat

herbivores—animals that only eat plants

mammals—warm-blooded animals that have backbones and feed their young milk

mates—partners

predators—animals that hunt other animals for food

ranges—the places where moose live

split hooves—hooves that are split into two toes; hooves are hard coverings that protect the feet of some animals.

underfur—an inner layer of short, soft hair that keeps moose warm and helps them float

To Learn More

AT THE LIBRARY

Albertson, Al. *White-tailed Deer*. Minneapolis, Minn.: Bellwether Media, 2020.

Borgert-Spaniol, Megan. *Moose*. Minneapolis, Minn.: Bellwether Media, 2016.

Pettiford, Rebecca. *Reindeer*. Minneapolis, Minn.: Bellwether Media, 2019.

ON THE WEB

FACTSURFER

Factsurfer.com gives you a safe, fun way to find more information.

1. Go to www.factsurfer.com.

2. Enter "moose" into the search box and click 🔍.

3. Select your book cover to see a list of related web sites.

Index

adaptations, 5, 8
antlers, 12, 13, 14
biome, 5
charge, 13
energy, 14
food, 11, 16, 17, 19, 20
fur, 7, 8
guard hairs, 7
herbivores, 16
legs, 6, 8
males, 12
mammals, 4
mates, 12
predators, 13
range, 5, 10

snow, 6
split hooves, 8, 9
spring, 12
status, 15
summer, 11, 14
swim, 9
teeth, 18, 19
travel, 10, 11
underfur, 7
winters, 6, 11, 14

The images in this book are reproduced through the courtesy of: Jack Bell, front cover (moose), p. 10; Artiste2d3d, front cover (foliage), p. 3; Valerii_M, front cover (background); Aleksey Stemmer, pp. 2-3; Michael Liggett, p. 4; Josef Pittner, p. 6; Ariel Celeste, p. 7; Martha Marks, p. 8; Ilkka Koivula, p. 8 (inset); Paula Cobleigh, p. 9; Gary George, p. 11; Aroha Miller, p. 12; genesisgraphics, p. 13; All Canada Photos/Alamy, pp. 14, 21; Paul Tessier, p. 15; Teri Virbickis, p. 16; chloe7992, p. 17; Szczepan Klejbuk, p. 18; Stefan Holm, p. 19 (left); ViralMind, p. 19 (right); North woodsman, p. 19 (bottom); m-kojot, p. 20; Steve Bower, p. 23.